How to Rock
Your Baby

For our respective children in order of appearance:
Vincent Schaum, "Wolfie" Schaum, and Jack Amoss.
And best wishes for Margaret Amoss,
the latest "rocker" on the scene.
—*S.F. and J.A.*

Published by
PEACHTREE PUBLISHERS, LTD.
494 Armour Circle NE
Atlanta, Georgia 30324

Text © 1997 by Sibley Fleming
Illustration © 1997 by John Amoss

Manufactured in China

10 9 8 7 6 5 4 3 2 1
First Edition

Library of Congress Cataloging-in-Publication Data

Fleming, Sibley.
    How to rock your baby / Sibley Fleming; illustrations by John Amoss. —1st ed.
        p.   cm.
    Summary: A new mother and father faithfully follow the instructions they get
for taking care of their new baby, but they get carried away when they try to rock the baby to sleep.
    ISBN 1-56145-142-8
    [1. Babies—Fiction. 2. Bedtime—Fiction.] I. Amoss, John, ill. II. Title.
    PZ7.F6228Ho 1997   96-41581
                                               CIP
                                             AC

How to Rock Your Baby

Words by Sibley Fleming
Pictures by John Amoss

PEACHTREE

ATLANTA

One day there wasn't a baby

and the next day
there was.

Baby came with a book that told...

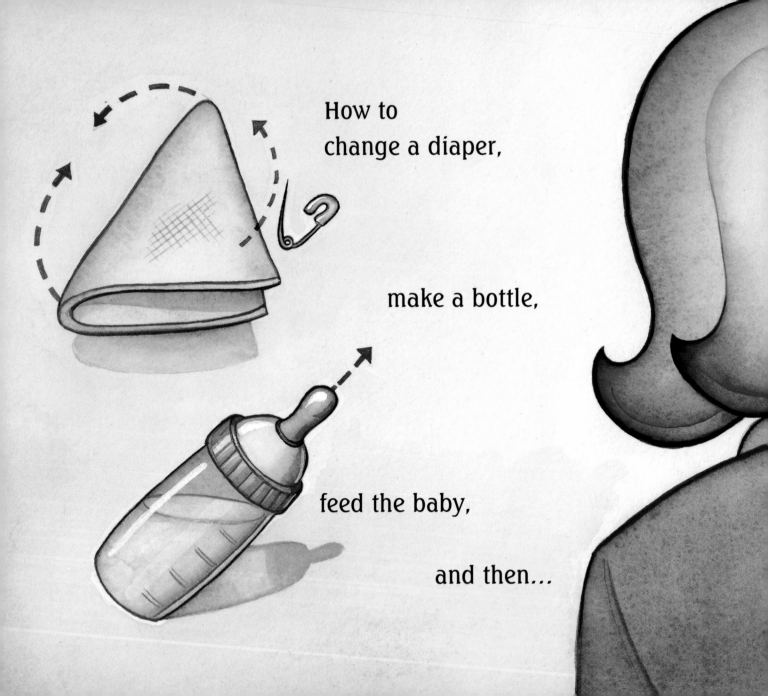

How to
change a diaper,

make a bottle,

feed the baby,

and then...

pat,
pat,
pat
the baby's back
until Baby
b-u-r-r-r-p-e-d
bubbles.

Last of all, the book said,
"Now rock the baby
to sleep."

"Cars rock," said the father,
"We'll drive the baby 'round the block."

So they drove 'round and 'round
and 'round the block,

past a
yellow moon...

and a tower clock.

But the car rocked too fast
to rock that baby to sleep.

"If that car won't rock," said the mother,
"We'll take the baby to the mountaintop."

So up

and up

and up

to the mountaintop they went

to watch their baby swing

over the World of Everything.

But the night
was too bright
to rock that baby to sleep.

"If that swing won't rock," said the father,
"We'll take the baby to the dock."

So they sailed out
        and out
              and out
                    to sea.

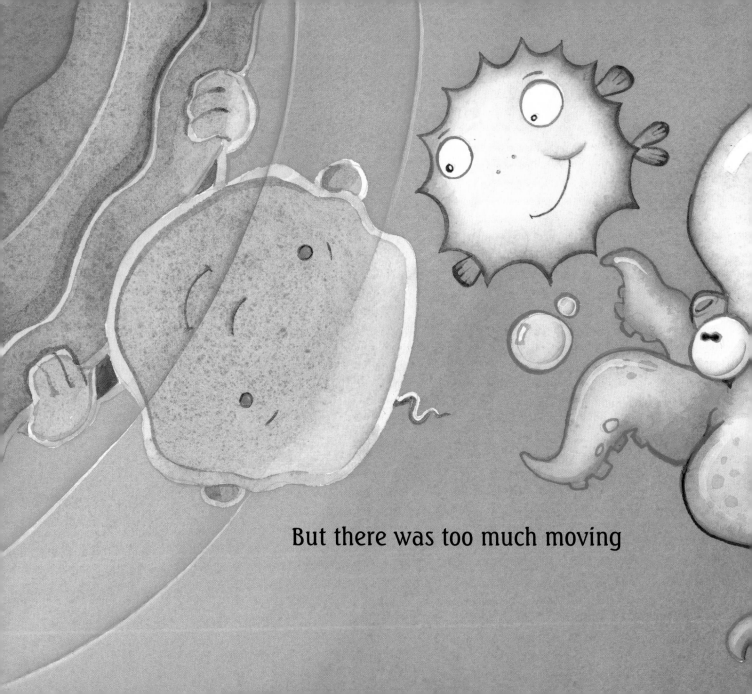

But there was too much moving

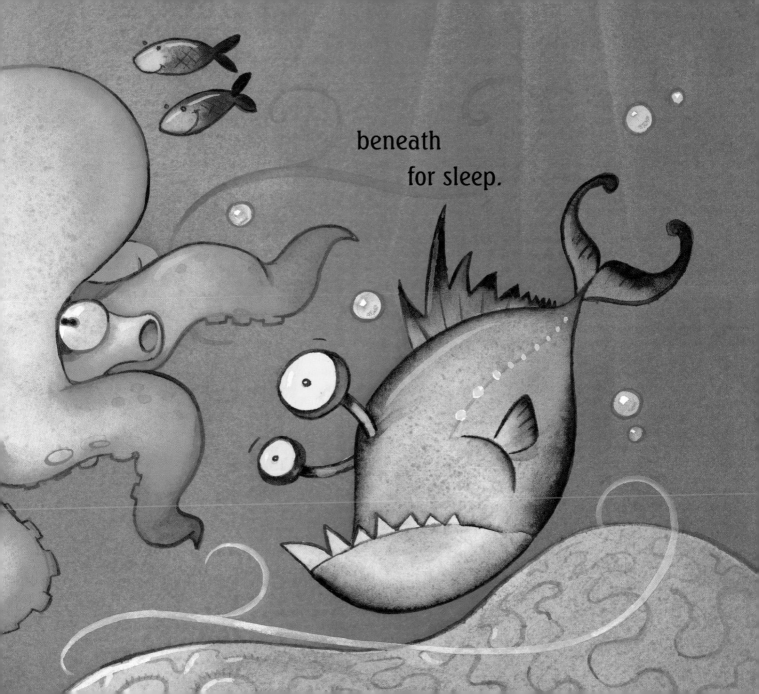

beneath
for sleep.

"If that boat won't rock," said the mother, "We'll take the baby to the park."

So down

and down

and down they went

to hear a lullaby.

The crickets crooned:

"Hush little baby,
   don't say a word,
Daddy's gonna buy you
      a mockingbird..."

But the lullaby
was too loud
to rock that baby to sleep.

And then the bells rang twelve strikes of the clock—
surely by now Baby should have been rocked!

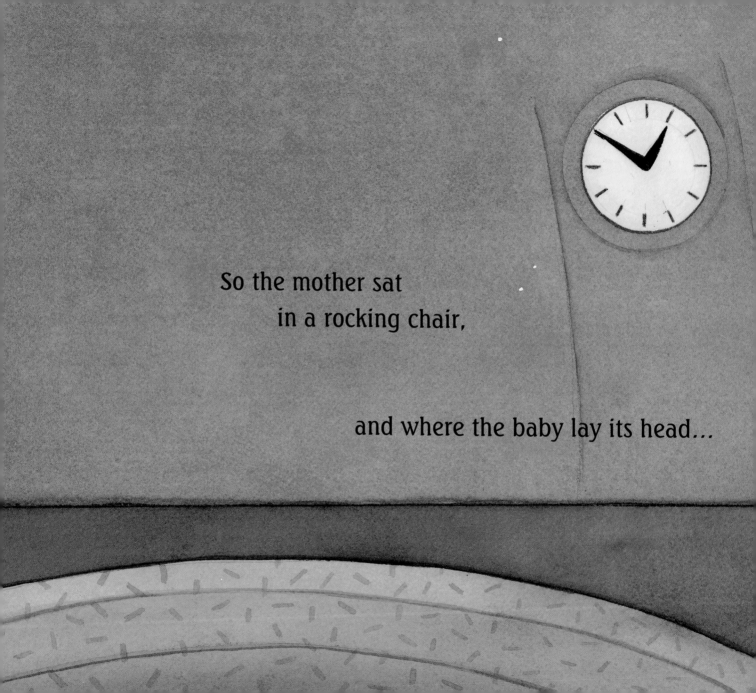

So the mother sat
in a rocking chair,

and where the baby lay its head...

beat her heart.

And she began to rock

back
and forth,

and back
and forth...

And for no reason at all
(or so it would seem)

Baby closed its eyes...

...and began to dream.